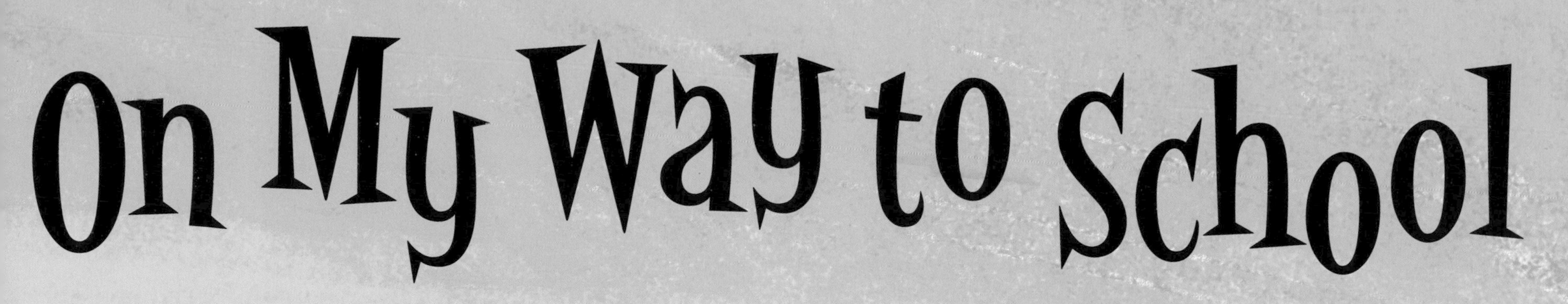

On My Way to School

Sarah Maizes

illustrated by

Michael Paraskevas

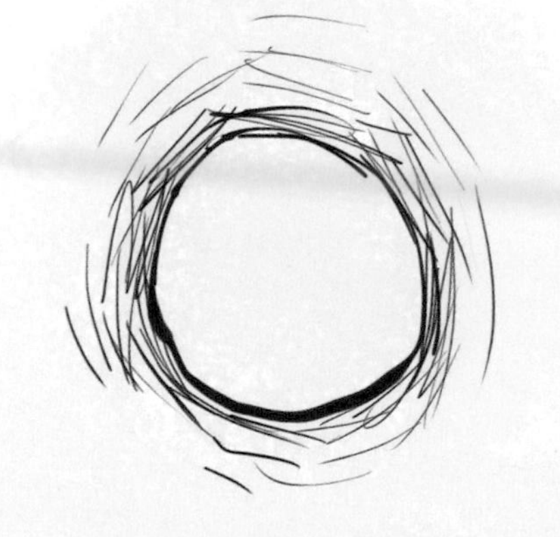

WALKER BOOKS FOR YOUNG READERS
AN IMPRINT OF BLOOMSBURY
NEW YORK LONDON NEW DELHI SYDNEY

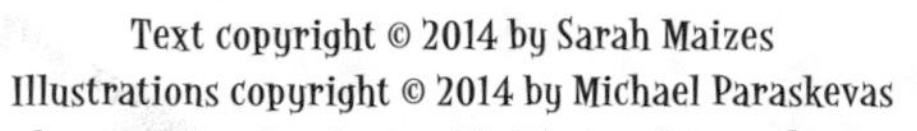

First published in the United States of America in July 2014 by Walker Books for Young Readers, an imprint of Bloomsbury Publishing, Inc.
www.bloomsbury.com
Bloomsbury is a registered trademark of Bloomsbury Publishing Plc

For information about permission to reproduce selections from this book, write to Permissions, Walker BFYR, 1385 Broadway, New York, New York 10018
Bloomsbury books may be purchased for business or promotional use. For information on bulk purchases please contact Macmillan Corporate and Premium Sales Department at specialmarkets@macmillan.com

Library of Congress Cataloging-in-Publication Data
Maizes, Sarah.
On my way to school / by Sarah Maizes ; illustrated by Michael Paraskevas.
pages cm
Summary: Livi imagines herself as an elephant, a Sherpa leading an expedition up Mount Everest, and a movie star signing autographs as she tries to avoid going to school.
ISBN 978-0-8027-3700-7 (hardcover) • ISBN 978-0-8027-3708-3 (reinforced)
ISBN 978-0-8027-3771-7 (e-book) • ISBN 978-0-8027-3772-4 (e-PDF)
[1. Schools—Fiction. 2. Imagination—Fiction.] I. Title.
PZ7.M279540ms 2014 [E]—dc23 2013039131

Art created digitally with a Wacom Cintiq tablet in Painter and Photoshop
Typeset in Boopee and Latino Rumba
Book design by Donna Mark and John Candell

Printed in China by Leo Paper Products, Heshan, Guangdong
2 4 6 8 10 9 7 5 3 1 (hardcover)
2 4 6 8 10 9 7 5 3 1 (reinforced)

All papers used by Bloomsbury Publishing, Inc., are natural, recyclable products made from wood grown in well-managed forests. The manufacturing processes conform to the environmental regulations of the country of origin.

For my mom. Now I understand.
—S. M.

To Derek and Lili for accepting me into their world and showing me a barking good time
—M. P.

Good morning! Time to get ready for school.

I do not want to go to school. School is for people who need to learn stuff. I have gone to school a hundred times, and I already know lots of stuff.

I will stay in bed.

On my way to school, I ooooooze out of bed.
I am a snail. I am slippery. I am slimy. I move
sooooooooO . . . slooooooWWWWWWWW . . .
across the floor.

Get dressed, please!

On my way to school, I dig through my drawers looking for underwear. **YO HO HOOOO**. I am a pirate digging for treasure, and Froggolini is me first mate. **YAARRGG!!** A scallywag has hidden me booty!

Come eat breakfast!

On my way to school, I see my brother eating oatmeal. Oatmeal is boring. I am a chef, and I will make triple-chocolate-chip pancakes for breakfast!

Your cereal is getting soggy.

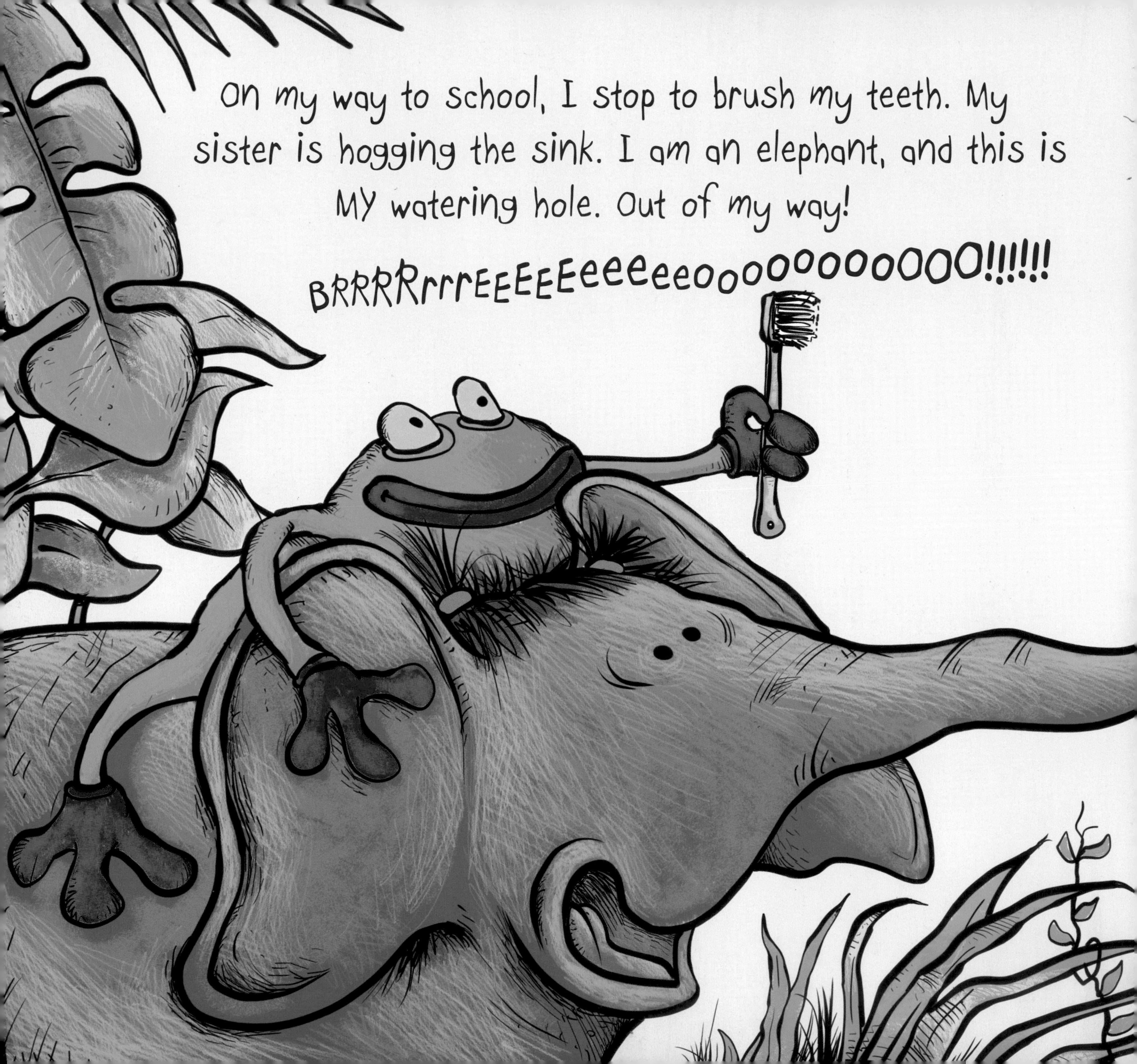
On my way to school, I stop to brush my teeth. My sister is hogging the sink. I am an elephant, and this is MY watering hole. Out of my way!
BRRRRrrrEEEEeeeeeoooooooooooO!!!!!!

There is enough room for both of you!

On my way to school, I lift my backpack. It is so heavy! I am a Sherpa, and I will lead a group of fearless explorers to the top of Mount Everest. We'll be gone for weeks and will have to live on potato chips and old turkey sandwiches . . .

Do you have everything?

On my way to school, I hop up and down the sidewalk on my hopscotch board. I am a kangaroo. I bounce, I bob, I boing. Everything I need is right in my front pocket.

The bus is here, Livi.

I am an Ol' Wild West woman crossing the open plains.
As I climb into my covered wagon, it's so hard to say good-bye. Who knows when we'll see each other again . . .

Get on the bus.
Have a great day.
SMOOCH!

I get on the bus. But I will not have a great day.

SCHOOL BUS

I see my best friend, Jonesy, and he saved me a seat! We are wild lemurs living deep in the jungle! We leap from tree to tree so we don't get eaten by hungry tigers below!

Sit down back there!

On my way to school, I sashay down the school-bus stairs. I am a movie star! I strut, I stroll, I wave to all my waiting fans. Hello! Why, yes, I'd be happy to sign some autographs!

Hurry up and get to class, please.

Hey, look! I'm student of the week! I'm practically a queen! I will rule the school! I proclaim everyone gets their own bunny—and four recesses a day.

Good morning, class! Let's begin!

I play, I share, I raise my hand a lot.

BRRRRRRING!
4
+5
9
2+3-1=
That's all for today.
Time to go home.
Livi?
Livi . . . ?

I am a teacher . . .

2+5=7